I've Got Chicken Pox

• WRITTEN AND ILLUSTRATED BY *True Kelley* •

DUTTON CHILDREN'S BOOKS • NEW YORK

to Jada Lindblom

with thanks to Dr. Christian Hallowell

and school nurse Pat Marsh

• • •

Library of Congress Cataloging-in-Publication Data
Kelley, True. I've got chicken pox/written and illustrated by True Kelley.—1st ed.
p. cm.   Summary: When Jess gets chicken pox it seems glamorous at first, but soon
she gets tired of being stuck at home.   ISBN 0-525-45185-4   [1. Chicken pox—Fiction.
2. Sick—Fiction.]   I. Title.   PZ7.K2824Iaad 1994   [E]—dc20   93-11685   CIP AC

Published in the United States 1994 by Dutton Children's Books,
a division of Penguin Books USA Inc.
375 Hudson Street, New York, New York 10014

Designed by Adrian Leichter
Printed in Hong Kong
First edition

3 5 7 9 10 8 6 4 2

I'm waving to my best friend, Anna. She's finally back at school today. She was out with the chicken pox.

She's so busy telling everyone what it was like, I hardly get to talk to her.

POX FACT: Chicken pox is easy to get from someone who has it or is coming down with it. But you cannot get it from someone who is over it.

In music class, Anna and I sit next to each other. Mr. Cox makes us all put our heads down on the table and listen to ballet music and smell the awful table smell.

POX FACT: The varicella zoster virus causes chicken pox. When an infected person breathes or coughs, the virus travels through the air on droplets, the way a flu virus does.

"I hate that smell. It's giving me a headache!" I whisper to Anna.

"That's how chicken pox starts," she says. She should know. She's the expert.

"Oh, well," I whisper, "I guess if I'm going to be sick, it might as well be something interesting."

If you breathe the droplets and catch chicken pox, spots will appear within three weeks. Soon before that, you may have a headache or fever, or feel tired.

After school, I change my clothes. There's a red spot on my tummy.

"Hey, Mark! I've got a chicken pock!" I yell to my brother.

"It's probably just a cootie bite," he says.

POX FACT: When spots first appear, often on your back or chest, they may look like bug bites. But they quickly become water blisters surrounded by a pink halo, and

The next morning there are spots on my arm, my chest, and my neck.

"Check these out," I say to Mom.

then develop into an itchy rash. Some of the virus is in the blisters, too.

"Oh, dear," she says. "It sure looks like chicken pox to me. I'm afraid you'll have to stay home. I'd better call the doctor."

"Yay!" I yell. "I've got chicken pox! No school! I can stay in my pajamas all *week!*"

 P O X   F A C T : If you think you have chicken pox, your doctor should be contacted. Most children have a fever and don't feel like eating. A child should *never* take aspirin,

"*Breathe* on me! *Breathe* on me!" says Mark.

as it could cause **Reye's syndrome, a very serious complication.**

Mark goes to school, and I get out my crayons and coloring books. Mom makes me put on a robe and slippers even though I hardly feel sick at all.

I fool around all day.

Mom lets me drink about a gallon of ginger ale and watch TV and listen to tapes all at the same time! I read to my animals until my eyes hurt.

and until about five days after the rash appears. When the spots are dry, you are no longer contagious.

When I wake up the next day, I have a sore throat. I feel so hot, and the itchy spots are everywhere. Even in my belly button!

"You've got spots on your tongue and in your throat, too," Mom says.

I stay in bed all day.

POX FACT: Cooling can reduce itching. Try wetting your skin; as the water evaporates, it will cool you. Or try smearing on calamine lotion or a baking-soda-and-water

After everyone else has supper, Mark brings me a piece of chocolate fudge cake, but I don't feel like eating it. So *he* does—right in front of me.

"Mmm, GOOD!" he says. "Want some?"

Dis-gus-ting!

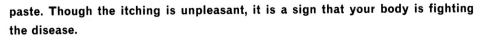
paste. Though the itching is unpleasant, it is a sign that your body is fighting the disease.

Oh, *itchy!* I don't even feel like watching Saturday morning cartoons. I just want to scratch.

Dad cuts my fingernails short.

Mom gives me a baking-soda bath.

I hate looking at my own tummy. Gross!

P O X   F A C T: You may get scars, called pockmarks, from chicken pox if you scratch too hard and damage your skin. So cut your fingernails short or wear mittens or gloves.

Sunday there are chicken pocks inside my cheeks. Dad brings me some Jell-O to make them feel better. I make that squishy Jell-O noise in my cheeks.

"Yuck!" Mark says. "Cut that out!"

To relieve pocks in the mouth, gargle with an eight-ounce glass of water containing one-half teaspoon of salt.

All night I scratch and scratch. "Mom! Dad! I can't sleep!"
Dad gives me an oatmeal bath. It is so weird. The house is

 POX FACT: For a soothing bath, add one-half to one cup of baking soda (or one-half cup of cornstarch or uncooked oatmeal) to one tubful of warm water. The itching may

dark and super-quiet, but the bathroom is too bright and my splashes are too loud. I hate chicken pox!

be worse during the bath, but you will feel better for hours afterward. Bathing does not spread the rash.

In the morning I feel a little better. At lunchtime Dad brings me a get-well present.

"You can have as much ice cream as you want," Mom says.

My aunt sends over a new book. Mom reads it to me.

POX FACT: If you get chicken pox and your brothers and sisters haven't had it, they will probably catch it from you. Unfortunately, the second child to come down with

Mark gets home from school. "*Breathe* on me! *Breathe* on me!"
he pleads.

"It'll cost you a dime," I tell him.

The next day, my teacher sends Anna over with some work-books. I don't feel like doing schoolwork, but I sort of miss the kids. Anna can't stay, because Mom says I need to rest.

 P O X   F A C T : To catch chicken pox you must be in close contact with someone who has it—as close as a few inches—because the virus, carried on the breath or on

Today I got a get-well card from Grandma and one from my class. Now I really miss all the kids. The school nurse told Mom I'm not allowed back for five more days. That's such a long time.

Mark says I don't know how good I've got it. Just before bedtime I breathe on him for five minutes for free.

moist sores, does not survive long outside the human body. It is not spread by dry scabs or on clothing.

One day down; four to go. I'm sick of TV. I'm sick of books. I'm sick of Jell-O.

I'm not sick of ice cream and ginger ale, though.

 POX FACT: The chicken pox blisters break, become crusty, and then turn to scabs. When you have the rash, you should wash your hands three times a day and gently

The thing I hate about chicken pox is the coloring. It's so pretty outside, and all I can do is color.

wash all over with soap and water daily to prevent bacterial infection.

I make a house out of pillows in the living room. I wish Anna could come over. I call her on the phone just to talk, but she's not home. She's playing at Kyla's house.

 POX FACT: Most people get between two hundred fifty and five hundred spots. But some may get only twenty; others, more than a thousand! The rash usually lasts

Believe it or not, I'm actually sick of ginger ale.

The house is horribly quiet.

"YAH YAH chickle pickle poxle doxle!" I yell. "I can't STAND it!"

The five days are almost up. My spots are fading, and I don't itch anymore. But Mom won't let me go out.

 P O X   F A C T: In many communities, kids can go back to school or day care two days after new pocks stop appearing, or about one week after the spots first appear. Some

"It's not fair!" I sob. "I feel like a prisoner. I'm *sick* of chicken pox!"

"Don't worry, Jess," Mom says. "You go back to school tomorrow."

schools make you stay at home until all the scabs are gone.

At last! Today I'm going back to school! *Hooray!*

 POX FACT: Most children get chicken pox between ages two and six. But you can get it at any age. It is more serious in adults than in children.

"I think I have a spot," says Mark.
"It's probably a cootie bite," I tell him.
"If it is, I caught it from you," he laughs.

At school, the kids seem almost like strangers. Even their voices sound different to me. "Hi, Jess!" they say. "How was the chicken pox?"

Everybody asks the same thing, except for Mark, who says, "How was the cootie pox?"

POX FACT: About four million Americans a year get chicken pox. Almost every American child gets chicken pox before age ten. Most cases occur in winter or spring.

I tell the kids about itching all night. I tell them about breathing on Mark for a dime. I tell them about how sick I got of ginger ale and coloring and TV and books. I tell them about the baking-soda and oatmeal baths and the Jell-O cheeks. I show them a pock scar on my arm. I tell them about pocks even on my tongue and in my throat.

"AWW, NEAT!" they say. "COOL!" "Luck-ee!"
"Yeah," I say, "it was *great!*"
Too bad you only get chicken pox once.

 POX FACT: Most people who get chicken pox won't get it again. Antibodies against the disease remain after you get well, and true second cases are rare.